Groundwood Books / House of Anansi Press
groundwoodbooks.com

We acknowledge for their financial support of our
publishing program the Canada Council for the Arts, the
Ontario Arts Council and the Government of Canada

Canada Council   Conseil des Arts
for the Arts   du Canada

ONTARIO ARTS COUNCIL
CONSEIL DES ARTS DE L'ONTARIO
an Ontario government agency
un organisme du gouvernement de l'Ontario

With the participation of the Government of Canada   Canadä
Avec la participation du gouvernement du Canada

Library and Archives Canada Cataloguing in Publication
Sadu, Itah, author
Greetings, Leroy / Itah Sadu ; illustrated by Alix Delinois.
Issued in print and electronic formats.
ISBN 978-1-55498-760-3 (hardback).
— ISBN 978-1-55498-761-0 (pdf)
I. Delinois, Alix, illustrator   II. Title.
PS8587.A242G74 2017   jC813'.54   C2016-906059-4
C2016-906060-8

The illustrations were done in acrylic and mixed media.
Design by Michael Solomon
Printed and bound in Malaysia

I give thanks to the Creator for
this gift and for all gifts.
To my sister Robin Anne Battle,
thanks for the challenge and
love to write this story.
To the young and dynamic
Solomon Higgins,
Jai'da Johnson, Ikebra Saul,
Berhan Saul and
the Ubuntu Drum & Dance
Theatre, thanks for the
inspiration and encouragement.
I see all the potential and
possibilities in your eyes. IS

To Ruby —
Dada and Mama love you. AD

Greetings,
Itah Sadu

Pictures by
Alix Delinois

Leroy

GROUNDWOOD BOOKS
HOUSE OF ANANSI PRESS
TORONTO   BERKELEY

Greetings, Leroy.

This is my third e-mail to you and I can't hear from you. Something bad happen to your hand? Is your computer not working? Write back to me, please, please, Leroy.

   Who won the cricket match? Anyone broke my score in soccer yet? How are the other Roys doing, Iroy, Delroy, Uroy, Stedroy, Buckroy and Royson? Tell them I said hi.

   Leroy, I want to tell you about my first day of school in Canada. I was so nervous the night before that I hardly slept.

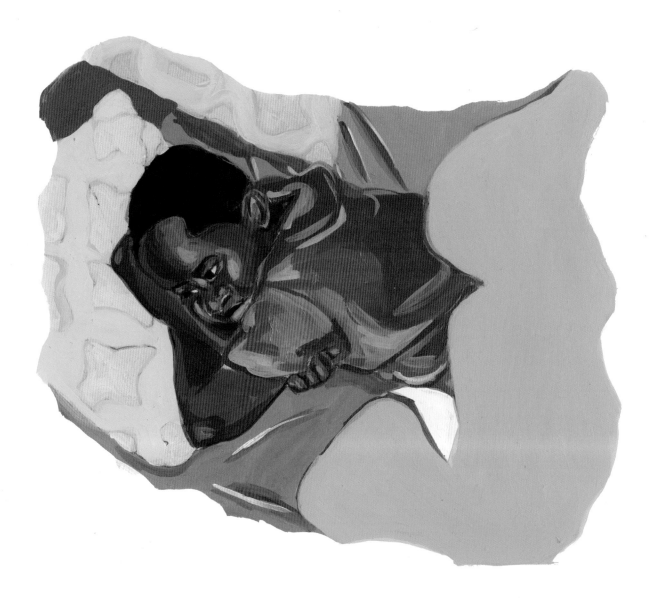

I woke up early in the morning, but my father, he woke up earlier than me. He was playing his favorite music, Bob Marley and the Wailers.

My father always say, "Roy, the Honorable Robert Nesta Marley's music is played every second, every minute, every hour everywhere, every day in the world. He is one of the greatest musicians the world has ever seen."

I could hear "Sun is shining, the weather is sweet, make you want to move your dancing feet."

Leroy, the sun was shining bright, bright outside, but when I put my head out the window, my ears felt a little cold. Some days I think the sun in Canada is cold.

As my mother and I left our home, the next-door neighbor, Ms. Muir, came up to me and said, "Roy, I have a special gift for you. I know you will wear it with pride." Ms. Muir then pinned a blue Bob Marley button on me. "Bob Marley was a great man," she said. "He brought people together. I bought this button when he gave a concert in my country, Ireland."

I puffed out my chest big, big and grinned from ear to ear, because Bob Marley was Jamaican and I am Jamaican, too.

At school, my mother took me to the principal's office. Oh my stars!! There was a picture of Bob Marley playing soccer. The principal saw me looking at it, and she said, "Roy, we have a great soccer team at this school. Do you like soccer? Maybe you will join the team one day. Bob Marley loved playing soccer."

What she said made me so excited that I took off my button, showed it to the principal and told her all about Ms. Muir and the gift she gave me for my first day at school in Canada.

My mother walked me to my class and introduced me to my
new teacher. I was so nervous looking at so many new eyes
staring at me. The teacher then said, "Students, let's welcome
Roy to the class."

The whole class stood and said, "Welcome, Roy, one love."

How did they know that "One Love" is one of my favorite
Bob Marley songs?

I was so happy with their greeting that I said to the class, "Look at my jacket!" But when they looked and I looked, I was pointing to an empty space on my jacket.

Where was the button? What happened to my Bob Marley button? Then I remembered I had left it on the principal's desk.

I asked for an excuse and ran all the way to the principal's office. My button wasn't there! The principal wasn't there! The secretary said she would be back soon.

"How long will she be?" I asked. I sat down and waited a lifetime in the office.

The principal soon
returned and we searched
up and down, high and
low and all around, but we
couldn't find the button.
All we found was an
umbrella.

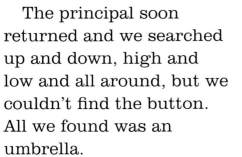

"Madame St. Fleur has
left her umbrella. Let's see
if she is still in the school,"
the principal said.

Madame St. Fleur was speaking with the secretary, while her baby giggled in its stroller.

"Thank you for finding my umbrella," Madame St. Fleur told the principal.

Just then the baby started rocking back and forth, shouting, "Yuck! Yuck!"

"We'll be leaving soon," Madame St. Fleur told the baby.

The baby yelled even louder, "Yuck! Yuck! Yuck!"

"Honey, I'm almost finished and then we're off home," Madame St. Fleur said.

But the baby screamed, "Yuck! Yuck! Yuck!"

Suddenly I thought of my baby sister, and I wondered what this baby was really trying to say. I rushed over to the baby and smiled. The baby shouted and bounced and wiggled like mad.

"Give me five!" I told the baby.

The baby stopped shouting and stared at me for a moment, and then slowly, slowly, very slowly, the baby shifted its bum in the stroller. There it was.

"It's my Bob Marley button under the baby's leg!" I shouted. I quickly picked up the button, thanked everyone, blew kisses at the baby and rushed back to my classroom.

16 + 9= 25

20+ 17= 37

52 + 13= 6

24 + 31=

44 + 11= 55

I showed all my new classmates my Bob Marley button. Some looked at it, some touched it, some played with it, some took pictures with it, and others even put it on. It felt like I was with you and all my friends in Jamaica.

Leroy, I felt very, very proud to know that one of the world's greatest and most caring musicians came from Jamaica and I am from Jamaica, too.

Leroy, I have typed you lots and lots of news. Please e-mail me soon, soon, and don't forget to say hi to all the other Roys. Nuff respect!

Your friend in Canada,
Roy